TILLY

Autumn Glory
the
new horse

TILLY'S PONY TAILS

Autumn Glory
the
new horse

PIPPA FUNNELL

Illustrated by Jennifer Miles

Orion
Children's Books

First published in Great Britain in 2011
by Orion Children's Books
a division of the Orion Publishing Group Ltd
Orion House
5 Upper St Martin's Lane
London WC2H 9EA
An Hachette UK Company

1 3 5 7 9 8 6 4 2

A catalogue record for this book is available from the British Library.

ISBN 978 1 4440 0092 4

Printed and bound in the UK by CPI Mackays, Chatham ME5 8TD

www.orionbooks.co.uk
www.tillysponytails.co.uk

For my very dear friends,
Chris and Dobby

The character of Tara in this story takes her name from
a real-life Tara, who is a member of The Pony Club.
Tara won a competition run through The Pony Club
to become a character in a Tilly's Pony Tails book.

To find out more about The Pony Club,
go to www.pcuk.org.

One

It was a pleasant spring evening and Tilly Redbrow was in the outdoor arena at Silver Shoe Farm, helping Angela with a beginner's lesson. It was the first time Angela had asked Tilly to give her a hand and Tilly was pleased that Angela thought she was good enough. Some of the riders seemed quite nervous, but Tilly was doing her best to make them feel better.

She knew the riding school ponies well, particularly Rosie, the sweet-natured

strawberry roan, whom she'd learned to ride on herself. There was also Aladdin, and Nimrod, the ex-circus pony. Each had their own personality but they all looked after their riders and walked calmly round the arena.

By the end of the session, everyone was smiling and looking proud. Tilly loved to see this. It reminded her of how far she'd come. When she'd first started helping at

Silver Shoe, she'd only ever dreamed about riding a horse. Now, with help from Angela, Silver Shoe Farm's owner, and Duncan, Silver Shoe's head boy, Tilly was a talented rider. And the horse she rode, of course, was Magic Spirit.

Tilly and Magic had been inseparable from the day they'd met. Tilly had helped rescue him from a busy roadside in North Cosford, and from that moment,

they'd bonded. Every day, she cleaned out his stable, fed and groomed him, and, best of all, exercised him. When she wasn't at the stables or out riding, she was thinking about him.

Tilly wore a bracelet made of Magic's tail-hairs, which matched the one her birth mum had given her before she was adopted. She always felt close to him, even when they were apart. Tilly liked to make tail-hair bracelets from all the wonderful horses she met and give them to her friends.

Just then, Tilly spotted her friend Mia walking towards her, arms folded. Unusually for Mia, she looked glum. Tilly was puzzled for a moment, and tried to work out what was wrong.

'Hey, Mia,' she called. 'How about a Silver Shoe special in the club room – hot chocolate with extra marshmallows?'

'Here you go,' said Tilly, stirring the three pink blobs that were floating in Mia's favourite Pony Club mug. 'Drink this, then tell me what's up.'

'I'm fine,' said Mia quietly.

They sat down on the squishy sofas.

'Come on, Mia,' said Tilly. 'It's not like you to be so down. What's on your mind?'

'Oh, I just wish I could find the right horse.'

Tilly had suspected as much. Mia had been trying to find her perfect horse ever since she'd grown too tall for her pony, Rosie. So far, she'd had no luck. The closest she'd come was with Nimrod, the ex-circus pony, who was lively and had lots of spirit to match Mia's own. But he was too small. She needed a horse she could grow up with.

'It feels as if I've been looking forever. I'm so fed up of borrowing rides or having to ask around to see which horse is available. I want a horse that will be my best friend, like you and Magic.'

Mia looked as though she was about
to cry. Tilly put an arm around her friend
and, sure enough, she let out a big sob.
Tears rolled down her cheeks. It was
horrible to see Mia so upset, but Tilly could
understand it. All her friends had their
special horses – she had Magic, Cally had
Mr Fudge, Brook had Solo, Cynthia had
Pickle. Even Angela and Duncan had their
number ones. For Angela, it was her old
event horse, Pride and Joy, and for Duncan,
it was the super-speedy racehorse, Red
Admiral.

'Hey,' said Tilly. 'I think the only way we're going to make you feel better is by making a plan. This weekend, let's do it! Let's make it our mission to find you the perfect horse. We'll look at every horse in the area if we have to.'

'My parents are busy. They won't be able to drive us anywhere. Besides, they're getting tired of taking me all around the country looking at horses.'

'Maybe Angela could help us? She'll know what you should look for in a horse.'

Tilly picked up a pile of horse and pony magazines.

'Let's start with these. There are always loads of good adverts in the back. If Angela's up for it, we can make some viewing appointments.'

'Hello. Up for what?'

The girls swung round. Angela was standing in the doorway, holding some bridles.

'Um, we were wondering perhaps if, um, you might be able to help us find Mia

a new horse this weekend? With all your expertise – and your driving licence!'

Angela laughed.

'Do you know what? I'd love to. Sounds like a nice change from riding lessons. I'll ask Duncan to cover them. I'd much rather be looking at new horses. Are there any good ones in those?'

She nodded towards the magazines.

'We've just started looking,' said Mia.

'But we're determined,' added Tilly. 'Somewhere out there, Mia, your ideal horse is waiting for you. Look at this one. Dark bay, named Toffee Pop, excellent temperament, natural mover.'

Mia smiled.

'He sounds nice. Thanks for doing this, Tilly. You're such a good friend.'

Two

On Saturday morning the girls met in the yard at Silver Shoe. They were very excited about their weekend's mission and had lined up several viewings from adverts they'd found in magazines. But first they had to do their usual duties of grooming, feeding and mucking out. Mia looked after Nimrod and Aladdin, while Tilly tended to Rosie and Magic.

'Good morning, boy,' she said, as she approached Magic's stable.

Immediately, his ears pricked up. He

walked over and nudged her cheek. His
eyes were full of affection.

'What a lovely greeting! I'm pleased to
see you too,' said Tilly. 'Wish me luck for
today, Magic. I'm helping Mia find a new
horse. Any tips?'

Magic shook his head.

'Not sure? Never mind. I suppose if
Mia can find a horse even half as wonderful
as you then she'll be happy.'

Magic seemed to like this comment. He
lifted his head and gave a proud nod. Tilly
laughed.

'Here,' she said, putting a hand into her
jacket pocket. 'This is for you.'

She gave him a mint, which was one
of his favourite treats, and stroked his
glossy grey neck. Just the sight of Magic
made Tilly feel happy. She couldn't wait
to take him for a ride that evening. He was
her dream horse, and sometimes it felt as
though they'd been meant to find each
other. She hoped the same thing would
happen for Mia.

An hour later, Tilly and Mia and Angela climbed into Angela's four wheel drive, ready to set off for their first viewing.

'What's the name of the livery yard again?' said Angela.

'Waltham Grange,' said Mia. 'We're going to see a dark bay, Welsh Section D, called Moto. It says here: 'Well bred gelding. Very flashy with super bold movement. Halter broken and handled. All rounder."

'Sounds promising. I know Waltham Grange. It's just on the other side of Cosford. We've had a few horses from there in the past. It has a good reputation.'

Angela turned the wheel and they pulled slowly out of the farm gates. It was a clear morning and the trees were just beginning to blossom. In a week or so the branches would be thick with blooms, then the petals would fall to the ground. Tilly always enjoyed riding Magic through the blossom confetti. This year, maybe Mia and her new horse would be joining them.

Waltham Grange was a small yard with only six stables. It was very pretty. The stables were built from stone and the grounds were surrounded by a white fence. They pulled into the yard and jumped out. A young woman came to greet them.

'Hi, I'm Elizabeth,' she said. 'I've been trying to call you, but I couldn't get through. You've come to see Moto, haven't you?'

Mia nodded, but she could tell by Elizabeth's face that something was wrong.

'I'm afraid you've been pipped to the post,' said Elizabeth. 'We sold Moto first thing this morning to a girl who lives locally. I'm so sorry. You've had a wasted journey.'

Mia sighed, and so did Tilly. She could feel Mia's disappointment. Angela tried to cheer things along.

'Not to worry,' she said. 'These things happen. Do you have any other horses we can look at, while we're here?'

'Well, I know one of our owners is thinking of selling. I'm not sure this horse is what you're looking for, though. She's nice-looking, and she would move well enough for dressage.'

Mia glanced at Angela.
'Can we?' she whispered.
'Come on then.'

The horse's name was Misty Morning.
She was beautiful, with a
shiny grey coat. Tilly and
Mia both gasped when
they saw her. Immediately
Mia imagined herself
proudly trotting out on
this elegant mare.

'There you go,' said
Elizabeth. 'She's got the
basics well established. If
you could fault her at all
you might say she was a
little long in the leg, but
really she just needs a
good rider to take her to
the next level.'

'That could be me,' said Mia, excited.

'What's her temperament like?' asked Angela.

Tilly was impressed that Angela was being cool headed and not getting side-tracked by Misty's beauty.

'Um, she's growing in confidence,' said Elizabeth.

'You mean she's a bit nervous?' said Angela frankly.

Mia wasn't paying attention to this part of the conversation. She was too busy admiring Misty.

'Can I stroke her?' she said.

'Sure,' said Elizabeth.

Mia leaned over the stable door and held out her hand. She beckoned Misty with a soft tutt, but Misty just moved to the back of her stable.

'Come on, girl,' she said encouragingly.

Mia was calm and patient, but still Misty wouldn't approach.

'You have a go, Tilly,' said Mia, disappointed. 'Horses always come to you.'

Tilly stepped forward. She looked sideways at Misty and made a quiet cooing sound. Misty pricked her ears a little, but Tilly could tell from the quiver of her body, and her tense posture, that she was terribly nervous.

'Maybe Misty isn't the right horse, Mia,' she said. 'She's lovely, but her character

22

is all wrong for you. Besides, you hate dressage.'

Mia sighed.

'I suppose you're right.'

'Oh well,' said Angela. 'Thanks for showing us. I hope Misty finds the right home soon. But I guess it's time for us to carry on searching.'

'You know,' said Elizabeth. 'If you aren't successful, my sister's selling a horse.

Here's her phone number. She lives over in Stitch Green. It's a bit of a drive, but you never know, it might be worth your while.'

'Thanks,' said Angela. 'We've got a few more people to see this weekend but we'll bear it in mind.'

She took the piece of paper with the number on, and passed it to Mia, who put it in her jacket pocket.

'Good luck,' said Elizabeth. 'I hope you find what you're looking for.'

Three

The next horse they visited was a 15.2hh
bay thoroughbred called Calypso. Mia had
been very excited when she'd found the
advert in the back of
Horse Trader magazine,
and now that they
were on the way to
see him, she began to
feel better about the
horses at Waltham
Grange.

'I love the name Calypso,' she said. 'It said in the advert that he has loose athletic paces and learns very quickly – and he can jump natural fences. Maybe he'll be an eventer?'

'Maybe,' said Angela. 'Let's think about that sort of thing once we've seen him.'

Tilly knew Angela was trying to stop Mia getting carried away too soon, but she also knew how hard it was for Mia. She was desperate to find a horse of her own.

'I think it's a left turn now,' said Angela. 'Yes, this is it. Angel Bridge Lane. Wow! There are some nice houses along here!'

As they drove down the road, Tilly and Mia stared out of the window. The houses were huge with big driveways. They pulled up at the house where Calypso lived and got out of the car.

'I'd love to live somewhere like this one day,' whispered Mia. 'Me and Calypso.'

Tilly smiled, and hoped things would go well this time. Angela rang the doorbell. A woman answered.

'Hi. We've come to see about the horse.'

'Oh,' said the woman. 'I'll show you through. They're out by the pool.'

'Pool?' Mia mouthed.

She and Tilly grinned at each other.

They followed the woman through the hallway to an enormous kitchen, which Tilly thought must be at least as big as the yard at Silver Shoe. They went out through some patio doors to where the owners, a middle-aged couple, were sitting at a table by a large swimming pool.

'Oooh!' said the woman, standing up. 'Of course! You've come to see Calypso.'

She slipped her feet into some diamante sandals and came to greet them. The man just gave a little wave.

'Come on down to the stables. My husband built them himself, you know. He has a construction business.'

'So, why are you selling Calypso?' asked Angela.

'Oh, Clippy belongs to my daughter. She was mad keen on horses for years,

but now she's gone off to university, she's not bothered any more. Between you and me, I'm hoping we can knock down those stables and build a hot-tub and sauna.'

Tilly didn't say anything but she knew what she'd rather have at the end of her garden.

'Here he is,' said the woman, as they approached the concrete building. Calypso had a large stable. He was at the back, pacing to and fro.

'He's gorgeous,' said Mia. Calypso's head was neat and Tilly thought he looked in much better proportion than Misty Morning. 'He's just what I'm looking for.'

'Yes, my daughter used to do shows and he was placed every time he went out. He's mostly thoroughbred with a touch of Connemara. We wanted the best for her, obviously.'

'Does he always do that?' said Angela.

'Do what?'

'Pace. Up and down like that. We call it box walking.'

'Sometimes,' said the woman, with a shrug.

'He's beautiful,' said Mia.

'Do you like him then?' asked the woman.

'I love him!'

'Great. I can see you riding him, you know. I think you'd look really good together. I always thought he was destined for the top, but my daughter just doesn't have time now she's got her studies and her boyfriend. Someone like you, maybe you could take him all the way.'

'Really? Do you think so?' said Mia, eyes wide.

Angela and Tilly exchanged glances. Tilly watched as Angela ran her hand across the door frame, where the wood had been chewed.

'I see he's a bit of a crib-biter.'

'Yes,' said the woman dismissively. 'I've never understood why he wants to do that. Disgusting, if you ask me.'

'Hmm,' said Angela. 'Perhaps he needs

more exercise. Horses often pick up the habit because they're bored. And if they suck in air when they crib-bite, you have to keep an eye out for bloating, as that can lead to colic. Call the vet if he shows any signs of pain, won't you?'

'Yes, but I'm sure he'll be fine.'

'Well, thanks for showing him to us. We'd better be off. We've got other horses to see.'

'But . . .'

Mia looked at her pleadingly. 'But Angela, we haven't finished here yet. I really like him.'

Angela shook her head. 'I'm sorry, Mia, but as well as being a danger to himself, young horses can quickly pick up these sorts of habits if they see an older horse like Calypso doing it. I don't want to encourage any crib-biting at Silver Shoe.'

Tilly put her arm around Mia's shoulders and whispered in her ear.

'I don't think he's the one for you, Mia. Come on, let's go. '

They trudged back to the car, barely noticing the pool and the fancy house as they went past.

'That sort of thing really irritates me,' said Angela, as she opened the car door.

'But he was stunning,' said Mia sulkily. 'Even when he was pacing up and down.'

'He was stunning,' said Angela. 'But he had some major stable vices. Irresponsible owners. There's so much more to owning a horse than meets the eye, and too many people don't know how to look after them properly. It's one thing to have a horse kept in stables, but it's another not to give him proper daily exercise, which I don't think they're doing now that their daughter is away. All those vices would plague you too, Mia, if you bought him.'

'All he needs is a big field,' said Mia. 'Silver Shoe has lots of pasture.'

'Sure,' said Angela. 'It's true many vices are caused by confinement and insufficient exercise, so more time at pasture can reduce or even eliminate them.

But that's only if they haven't become well-established. Something tells me Calypso's vices have been around for a while. I'm sorry to say it, but long-term this behaviour can lead to all kinds of health problems. The cribbing may have damaged his teeth and that repetitive pacing will have placed unnatural stress on the legs. You don't want to buy a horse only to discover he's lame.'

'I suppose not,' said Mia.

'Don't worry' said Tilly. 'We've got more appointments lined up for tomorrow. Come on, Mia. Your horse could be just around the corner!'

Four

Early that evening, the girls returned to
Silver Shoe. Tilly was keen to give Magic
some extra exercise, especially after seeing
poor Calypso. She knew the horses at Silver
Shoe were lucky. Angela did what was best
for them. They were very well looked after.

Mia helped Tilly get Magic tacked up.
Tilly put the bit in Magic's mouth and
slipped the bridle over his ears. Then she
placed the numnah on, while Mia followed
it with the saddle. They tightened the

girth, checked everything, then Mia gave
Tilly a leg-up.

'Duncan's put up some jumps in the
sand school. He's over there now. Why
don't you have a go? I'll be your assistant!'

'Good idea.'

When they reached the sand school,
Tilly could see that the jumps Duncan had
set up were quite challenging.

Tilly was excited. She and Magic
had spent a lot of time with
Angela and Duncan building
their confidence over single
fences or grids, but they'd
never jumped a complete
course together.

As she warmed
Magic up, Duncan and Mia
adjusted some of the
jumps.

'Duncan, do you
think you could pull
that oxer in so it's a bit
narrower?' said Tilly.

36

'I think Magic might spook at the spotted filler. He hasn't seen it before, and I don't want him to land on the back rail.'

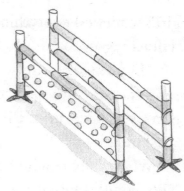

'Sure,' said Duncan. 'That's one of the reasons Tilly is so good,' he said, turning to Mia. 'It's not just about how well you ride, it's thinking about your horse, constantly assessing his level, and trying to avoid getting into a situation where you might frighten him, or risk losing his confidence.'

Once they'd warmed up, Tilly and Magic jumped the cross pole a couple of times, before Duncan moved it so that it was straight across. Tilly concentrated on keeping a consistent rhythm,

and worked on sitting as quietly as she could, remembering to keep her legs close to Magic's sides.

'Now try the spotted filler, but remember not to ride it any differently. Just be ready with your leg to give him a bit of a nudge if he does suddenly spook at it,' said Duncan.

'Okay,' called Tilly.

Tilly and Magic approached the jump. Magic was calm until he noticed the strange-looking fence covered in spots. Luckily, thanks to Duncan's advice, Tilly was ready with her leg and gave him a big, confident kick at the right moment, encouraging him forward. 'It's okay, it won't hurt you, boy,' she murmured.

Magic made an enormous jump, landing on all fours, and shifting Tilly out of balance.

'You were right, Tilly,' said Mia. 'If that oxer had been any wider, Magic would have landed on the back rail and frightened himself.'

'Don't come any quicker next time,'
said Duncan. 'Let him have time to see
what he's looking at.'

After a couple more goes, Duncan
pulled the fence wider and raised it up a
little. 'Right, I think you're ready to jump
the whole course now,' he said.

Tilly and Magic jumped smoothly and effortlessly around the set of fences.

'Clever boy!' she said, walking him over to Mia and Duncan.

'Looking good!' said Mia.

'Very neat,' agreed Duncan. 'You kept your hands really low and relaxed then.'

'That's a tip you gave me,' said Tilly. 'I don't always do it. Sometimes my arms get really tense and then I think about it too much and it makes it worse.'

'Seems like you did it without thinking just then.'

'I did, didn't I?'

Tilly smiled to herself. Angela always said confidence was the key to good jumping. A horse was far more likely to refuse or knock poles down if its rider wasn't convinced they'd make it.

While Tilly gave Magic a walk and a breather, Duncan and Mia put all the fences up a couple of holes.

'Wow! That was some mega-big jumping! If you keep that up, you'll be heading for the county horse shows!' said Mia when she'd finished.

'It was so much fun,' said Tilly, elated.

She patted Magic on the shoulder.

Mia was smiling but there was something else in her expression. Tilly knew she was wishing she could have a go at the jump herself.

'Do you want a turn?' she said. 'I'm sure Magic would be up for another try.'

Mia shook her head.

'You know Magic only performs for you,' she said. 'If I got up there he'd ignore me and refuse.'

This was true. Magic could be very stubborn unless Tilly was the one working with him.

'It's not fair,' said Mia, with a sigh. 'You guys have such an amazing connection. I need to find a horse I can bond with, but every time I see one I like, Angela finds something wrong with it.'

'It will happen,' said Tilly. 'But you should listen to Angela's advice. She knows

so much about these things and she's not going to let you walk away with a horse that isn't right for you.'

'I guess not,' said Mia.

'Don't worry,' said Tilly. 'We'll find one!'

Five

On Sunday morning, the girls had an
appointment in the next county, to see
a skewbald Irish sport horse called Rio.
They'd seen him advertised on the *Horse*
magazine website.

'Now, he sounds really good,' said
Mia, as they buckled their seatbelts.
'He's the perfect height for me. And it
says here, he's a quality all-rounder.
He never spooks and has good flat work
and a nice jump.'

'What's the name of the dealer?' asked Angela.

'Mr Antony Mason. It says he's highly experienced and has one of the best reputations in the area. There's a photo of him on the advert. He's got really white teeth.'

'Antony Mason? I haven't heard that name before.' She sounded slightly concerned. 'Oh well, we'll give it a shot, shall we?'

They arrived at Mason's Livery with plenty of time to spare. There was a silver convertible sports car in the car park.

'Nice!' said Mia.

The stable block itself was shaped like a large horseshoe, painted cream, and surrounded by fir trees. They spotted Antony Mason in the yard, but he was too busy talking on his mobile to notice them. Tilly and Mia didn't mind – it gave them a chance to check out some of the horses, whose heads were bobbing over the stable doors. Only a few of the stables were occupied. For a big livery yard it seemed very quiet.

'Ahem,' said Angela eventually.

Antony Mason turned and waved at them. It took him a minute to finish his phone conversation before he came over.

'Ladies!' he said.

'Hi,' said Angela. Tilly noticed the suspicion in her voice. 'We're here to see a horse – Rio.'

'Oh, that's right I spoke to one of you on the phone. You'll find what you want at Mason's, I guarantee you. If people round here want a good horse, they know they just have to come to me. Twenty years of horse trading experience is what it's all about. Do you lovely ladies know much about our four-legged friends?'

'Um, a bit,' said Tilly, smiling

'And Rio sounds like the sort of horse we're looking for,' said Mia.

'Well, if I may say so, you've got good taste. If I was buying a horse for my own daughter, Rio would be the one. I'll warn you now though, we've had a lot of interest in that fella. In fact, I've had a few offers

just this morning, so if you like him, you'd better move swiftly.'

'Oh,' said Mia anxiously. 'Can we see him then?'

'Sure.'

Antony Mason led Angela, Tilly and Mia over towards the far stable, where Rio

was waiting patiently. He was mostly white with brown splodges on his hindquarters and shoulders. He had a sweet face, and was immediately interested in Tilly and Mia when they approached him.

'He certainly likes you, girls,' said Antony Mason. 'That gives me a good feeling. I want my horses to go the people who'll love them. If you are interested, I'll give you priority for that very reason.'

Tilly thought she saw Angela roll her eyes slightly. She understood why. There was something about Antony Mason's smooth manner that wasn't quite right. Meanwhile, Mia grinned and stroked Rio's nose.

'What do want him for?' said Antony Mason.

'Everything,' replied Mia. 'I want to have my own dream horse. I'd really like to jump with him, so I can go to competitions and maybe even have a chance of winning something some day.'

'Oh, if jumping's your thing, he's ideal. Really powerful. You should see how big he

47

can jump. It's awesome. If anything, I'd say he's only good for an experienced rider. He clears heights you wouldn't believe.'

'Wow!' said Mia.

'In that case,' said Angela. 'I think it would be really useful if the girls could have a ride and see for themselves. They're both very competent in the saddle. Would that be possible?'

'Of course,' said Anthony Mason, flashing his white teeth. 'I'll get one of the helpers on to it. If you'll excuse me, I've got a few phone calls to make.'

One of the stable hands led Rio outside and tacked him up. As the girls stood watching, Angela immediately noticed a problem.

'There's no way that horse can jump,' she said. 'Antony Mason was making it all up.'

'What do you mean?' asked Tilly.

'Look at his hind legs. They're so far out behind him, he'd never have the power to push. He's a sweet-looking thing but he isn't a jumper.'

'Well, maybe he'll go okay when I actually ride him,' said Mia optimistically.

Tilly frowned, worried her friend was heading for another disappointment. They led Rio to the sand school. It was much smaller than the one at Silver Shoe. The stable hand set up a couple of jumps, a cross pole and a low vertical.

Mia got ready to mount. She swung her leg over and adjusted her position in the saddle.

'He feels great,' she exclaimed, and began circling the sand school to warm him up.

After a few laps, they approached the cross pole. They jumped it clear but it was obvious from the look on Mia's face that Angela's observations were accurate.

'There's just no oomph,' she moaned. She didn't even bother to try the next jump. Crestfallen, she dismounted.

'Have a go if you like,' she said, handing the reins to Tilly. 'But Angela's right.'

Curious to see for herself, Tilly mounted. She took Rio over the cross pole and then the vertical, but she could feel it intensely.

There was no spring in his legs, no thrust.
It was like jumping through wet sand.

'Just goes to show,' said Angela, shaking
her head. 'When you're buying a horse you

need to be thorough. Never take someone's word for it. Come on, girls, let's go and tell Antony Mason we won't be making a deal with him today.'

Six

'Don't worry, Mia,' said Tilly. 'We've still got one more horse to see this afternoon.'

She waved the advert under her nose. Mia took it and read.

'Oh, I don't know,' said Mia, despondent. 'I think I'm going to give up hope.'

'But check this out: an unnamed thoroughbred filly, four years old. Chestnut. Will be a brilliant horse in the right hands. Sad sale due to lack of time. What do you think?'

'Let's go and see,' said Angela. 'The dealer is an old friend of mine. She's very reliable, but with a young horse, there could be challenges. Sometimes an older, experienced horse is a safer bet.'

'But Magic wasn't an experienced horse,' said Mia. 'And look how well Tilly has done with him.'

'True,' said Angela. 'But what's happened between those two is quite unique. It was obvious from the start that they'd bonded, but that doesn't always happen.'

Tilly blushed and felt very proud. She thought about the moment she'd first approached Magic. She hadn't known what she was doing. She'd just followed her instincts.

They arrived at the livery yard with twenty minutes to spare before their appointment.

'Being early gives us a chance to go and see the filly in the field,' said Angela.

There was no one in the stable yard, which appeared to be well-kept and tidy, so they made their way to the fields at the back, where a few horses were grazing.

'Which one do you think it is?' said Mia, leaning over the fence.

There were two chestnuts, a bay and a grey.

'I think it's the bigger one,' said Tilly. 'That other chestnut is only a pony. The one you've come to see is 15.2hh.'

'Pretty accurate,' said Angela. 'You've always been good at judging horses' heights, Tilly.'

'Here, girl,' said Mia, trying to beckon the filly over.

The horse didn't respond. She kept her head in the grass and swished her tail. Tilly noticed she was keeping her distance from the other horses. Her ears were pinned back, which Tilly knew was a sign of aggression.

Eventually, the owner came over. She was a woman of about Angela's age, dressed in a quilted jacket and riding boots.

'Angela!' she said, smiling. 'How are you?'

'Great. How are you? Girls, meet Sarah Hopkins. Sarah, this is Tilly and Mia, two of my most talented young riders.'

'I see you're admiring our filly,' said Sarah. 'We've nicknamed her Queenie.'

'Why Queenie?'

'Because she likes to be in charge. Are you interested in her for yourself?'

Sarah looked at Angela.

'Oh no, this one's for Mia,' she replied.

Sarah studied Mia for a moment.

'Hmm. Have you done a lot of riding?'

'Yes. I've kept a pony for years. Now I'm looking for my first horse. Me and Tilly, we ride every day.'

Tilly nodded.

Sarah sighed. 'I don't want to put you off, but I think it's only fair to be honest. I'm not sure I'd recommend Queenie as a first horse.'

Mia frowned.

'I've ridden young horses before,' she protested. 'I know what to expect.'

'It's not just her age,' said Sarah. 'To be honest, she's got a bit of an attitude. From day one, she's been difficult. You can see it in her face, the way her ears are slightly pinned back. And this is Queenie being calm. Yesterday she gave one of our grooms a nip. We're hoping we can find someone with a lot of time and experience to take her on, someone who wants a challenge. She's got the potential to be fantastic. Her parents were both champions.'

Mia looked at Angela.

'Oh no,' said Angela. 'I've got enough horses to deal with already.'

'Champion potential,' said Sarah.

Angela shook her head.

'Well, I'm sure you're a very talented rider, Mia, but, frankly, I'd have sleepless nights if you went home with Queenie. I wouldn't want to hear that she'd bucked you off or done you an injury.'

'I suppose that's that then,' said Mia. 'We might as well go home.'

She sounded more upset than ever. When they got to Angela's car, Tilly could see Mia was fighting back tears. She gave her a hug, but she knew it wasn't enough to cheer her friend up.

Seven

Over the next week, Tilly tried her best to lift Mia's spirits, showing her the latest adverts in *Pony* magazine or online, and encouraging her to make appointments. But it seemed as though Mia had completely lost interest. She moped around the yard, performing her duties, but barely talking to anyone. By the following Sunday, even Duncan and Angela were beginning to lose patience.

'Can't you do something with her?'
Duncan asked Tilly, as they watched Mia
walking slowly towards the club room after
a lesson. 'Take her for a hack – anything to
put a smile on her face!'

'Come on, Mia,' called Tilly firmly.
'Magic needs some exercise. Why don't you
ride Watson?'

Mia paused, then nodded reluctantly
and followed Tilly down to the long field.

'What's that?' said Tilly. They'd just
finished tacking up their horses in the yard.

'Oh,' said Mia in surprise. She'd pulled
a scrap of paper from her jacket pocket.
'It's that phone number the woman at
Waltham Grange gave us the other day,
about the horse in Stitch Green. I'd
forgotten all about it.'

'Do you think it might be worth
calling?' said Tilly.

60

'I don't know,' said Mia, crumpling it up. 'Anything could have happened since last weekend. That horse has probably been sold by now, knowing my luck.'

Tilly took the paper from her and straightened it out.

'Call,' she said. 'You never know.'

Mia sighed and took out her phone. She dialled the number. It rang a few times before a girl answered.

'Hello?'

'Hi. Do you have a horse for sale?'

'You mean Autumn Glory? Yes. Are you interested?'

'We'd like to come and see him if we can.'

'Sure,' said the girl. 'You'll have to make an appointment.'

'Can we come today?'

'Oh. I'm afraid my mum's not in and it's her you really need to speak to. I'd show him to you myself, but I've got loads of horses to exercise, so I'll be busy for the rest of the day. Could you come tomorrow after school? About five o'clock?'

Mia glanced at Tilly. 'Tomorrow?' she mouthed.

'Maybe Angela could take us?' said Tilly. 'I'll check.'

She saw Angela coming out of the tack room, and ran over to explain what they were planning. Tilly turned back to Mia and gave her a thumbs-up.

'Okay. That sounds fine. See you then.'

'Great. See you tomorrow,' said the girl.

Mia shut her phone. She smiled at Tilly.

'I've got a good feeling about this one,' said Tilly, nudging her.

'I don't know,' said Mia. 'Anything could happen. What if Autumn Glory gets sold? What if he goes lame? What if he's a rubbish horse anyway? All the other horses I've seen have turned out to be wrong!'

'That's horse buying for you,' said Angela, joining them. 'As my dad always says, you've got to kiss a lot of frogs before you find a prince. The right horse is out there somewhere, but he won't just appear in front of you. You have to search for him.'

Tilly didn't say so, but she wasn't sure she agreed with Angela this time. It was as if Magic had just appeared in front of her. There had been no searching involved. She'd felt the connection instantly. But she knew this wouldn't help Mia feel better.

'Come on,' she said. 'Let's go for that ride.'

'Hey, boy,' Tilly whispered, as she walked over to where Magic and Watson were waiting patiently. Mia had wanted to call her parents quickly about tomorrow's horse

viewing. 'Ready for some exercise? We thought we'd go up the lane and back. It's lovely with all the spring flowers out.'

Magic nuzzled her shoulder. Tilly could see he was keen to get going.

'It looks like Mia might have another chance at finding her horse!' she said, untying him. 'Remember I told you we were going to find her a new horse last

weekend? Well, we saw some good ones and some not so good ones. It definitely made me realise what a lovely place Silver Shoe is – not that I didn't know already. There was this one horse, a huge bay called Calypso, or Clippy, as his owner called him. Angela noticed immediately that he had loads of stable vices. He was pacing up and down and he'd chewed the door to bits.'

Magic let out a soft wicker. Tilly patted his shoulder and smiled.

'Yes, you're a good boy, Magic. You don't have any vices, but that's because at Silver Shoe you have lots going on and plenty of exercise. Plus you've got other horses around you for company. Poor Calypso was all on his own and of course there was no way his owners were going to let him graze on their perfectly mown garden lawn!'

Seeing Mia emerge from the club room, she mounted and tightened Magic's girth.

'I'd love to bring all the horses we've seen back to Silver Shoe. They'd be happy here, that's for sure. Too many horses and not enough good homes. I wish there was something more I could do.'

With that Tilly nudged Magic to walk on.

Eight

Next day after school, Tilly and Mia raced to meet Angela at the gates. They were normally met by Mia's mum, so it was nice to see Angela waiting for them.

The journey to Stitch Green took longer than expected, along winding country lanes.

'This had better be worth it,' said Mia. 'I'm starting to feel car sick.'

'Nearly there,' said Angela. 'The road to the farm should be coming up on the right.

Keep an eye out.'

'There it is!' said Tilly. She'd spotted
a little wooden sign with an engraving of a
horse on it.

Angela swung
the car into the
turning and they
bumped along an
overgrown track.
The house was at
the end of it, in a

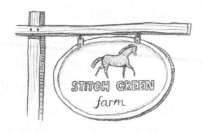

little valley surrounded by trees. It was very
pretty and peaceful. In the distance she
could see several large fields with horses
grazing in them.

As they pulled into the driveway, a
young girl came to greet them. She had
straight, shiny hair and sparkling brown
eyes.

'Hi, I'm Tara,' she said, in a warm,
friendly voice. 'We spoke on the phone.'

The girls introduced themselves.

'You've come to see Autumn? He's a
great horse. If you love him half as much

as I do, then he'll make you very happy.
I wish we didn't have to sell him, but
my mum always says we'll never make a
business out of breeding horses if we can't
bear to part with them.'

'Was he bred here?' asked Angela.

'Yes. We raised him from birth. His
parents were successful show jumpers, so
he's from good stock. We've bred and sold
quite a few horses, but Autumn is different.
He feels like one of the family.'

'That's so nice,' said Mia.

'Let's go and see him. He's in the field
– his favourite place. By the way,' she said,
looking down at Tilly's wrist. 'I love your
bracelets. That's horsehair, isn't it?'

'Yes.'

'Tilly makes them,' explained Mia. 'Out
of the tail-hairs of special horses. Look, I've
got one too.' She held up her wrist for Tara
to see.

'They're great.'

There were several horses in the field, but Autumn Glory stood out immediately. He was a well put together 15.2hh with a bronze sheen to his glossy chestnut coat. The name suited him. Tilly thought he was the colour of a conker. He looked athletic, with good conformation and clean limbs, and a short, strong back. Tilly glanced at Angela. She was smiling and nodding – she obviously approved.

Tara approached the fence and held out a hand.

'Autumn!' she called. 'Hey, boy! You've got visitors!'

Autumn pricked his ears and trotted over. He looked at the four faces admiring him from the fence, then went first to Mia. She couldn't believe it.

'Did you see that? Did you see? He's come straight to me! Hello, boy!'

Mia rubbed his nose and stroked his face, and he responded by nuzzling her neck.

Tilly was pleased. After all the bad luck,

it seemed as though something was finally going right.

'He likes you,' said Tara. 'I can see it. He's very good natured. He can be a bit of a cheeky boy at times, but only in a playful way. In terms of skill, he's done a bit of everything, but jumping has come through as his strongest. What do you like doing?'

'Jumping,' said Mia, with a grin.

'Why don't you have a ride?' said Tara.

Mia helped Tara get Autumn's tack on, while Angela talked to Tara's mum, who'd come out to meet them. Autumn obviously didn't mind having lots of people fussing over him. In fact, he seemed to love the attention. Tilly couldn't help admiring his beautiful shiny coat. She ran her hand across his hindquarter and combed her fingers through his tail, collecting the loose hairs as she went.

When Autumn was ready, Mia did up the strap on her crash helmet (she was already wearing her lucky jodhpur boots) and mounted. They walked up a path to a well-used sand school, where Mia worked him through his paces. After twenty minutes, it was obvious neither of them wanted to stop. Tilly was desperate to have

a go herself, especially because Angela was being very complimentary.

'He's a natural mover,' she said. 'He's got quite a long stride for a relatively small horse, and you've done a great job producing him, Tara.'

'We've done our best. We make sure none of the horses here are rushed, so they're all very confident and happy in

their work, and they get as much time in the field as possible. It's hard work, but it's worth it.'

'Do you ride a lot?' asked Tilly.

'As much as I can,' said Tara. 'I'm a member of The Pony Club and it's such good all-round grounding. I've learned so much about general horse management and care from doing The Pony Club Tests, and we have a brilliant instructor who's very knowledgeable about young horses. I love being in all their teams, and I've met so many good friends.'

At last Mia returned to the fence.

'I love him,' she said. 'He's lovely to ride.'

'Please,' said Tilly. 'Can I have ride too?'

'Of course,' said Tara.

Tilly put her hat on. She placed her left leg in the stirrup and swung her right leg over. As soon as she was secure in the saddle she could tell how different he was to Magic. His back was wider and her legs were more stretched. He was just as responsive though. She nudged him with her calf and he walked on.

As Mia had said, Autumn was very comfortable to sit on. Each stride seemed effortless. She couldn't wait to feel how he jumped. Tilly was sure Mia had finally found the right horse, she just hoped everything would work out. She could tell Mia was thinking the same. There was a happy/anxious look on her face. Tilly brought Autumn to a standstill, dismounted and led him back to the yard to be untacked, then went over to Mia.

'Are you okay?' she whispered.

'He's perfect,' said Mia. 'But I'm so worried it will fall through like the other horses have done. Maybe, if we decide to buy him, Angela's vet, Brian, will discover there's something wrong with his health, or he'll turn around out of the blue and bite me. Or somebody will buy him before I can get my parents to approve. I don't know.'

'Stay positive,' said Tilly. She squeezed Mia's shoulder. 'You just need to tell

Tara that you're one hundred per cent interested and then get your parents along here as soon as possible. It will all be fine, I promise.'

And as she said this Autumn bobbed his head.

'There you go – he agrees with me!'

Nine

That night Tilly went to bed early. She was exhausted after a busy day at school followed by the journey to Stitch Green. She thought she'd hit the pillow and fall asleep immediately, but instead her mind began to whirl, wondering and worrying and hoping it would all work out for Mia and Autumn Glory.

She knew there was no guarantee until it actually happened. This one felt perfect though. It had to happen. And she'd

already collected hairs from his tail. She remembered they were in the pocket of her cream jodhpurs, so she climbed out of bed and brought them over.

The hairs were a deep copper colour and very strong. She twiddled them around her fingers and pulled them into tight plaits. There was enough hair to make two bracelets. She got out her phone and texted Mia.

HEY. STILL AWAKE. LET ME KNOW WHAT UR PARENTS SAY ABOUT AUTUMN. X

A few minutes later, Mia replied.

CAN'T SLEEP EITHER. 2 EXCITED.
M & D HAVE AGREED 2 C AUTUMN 2MORROW. X

Tilly smiled. That was a step in the right direction at least. Now all it took was for Mia's parents to agree what a wonderful horse Autumn was. Tilly knew buying a horse was a big investment. She was lucky that she got to ride Magic all the time

and hadn't had to pay for him. Angela was
happy for Tilly to ride him in exchange
for all her help around the stables. And as
Duncan always said, if Tilly didn't ride him,
he wouldn't let anyone else! She texted
Mia again.

HOPE THEY SAY YES! XX

Mia replied:

ME TOO. SICK WITH NERVES! X

Tilly placed the phone back on her
bedside table, turned over and tried to sleep.
She realised she wasn't just thinking about
Mia and Autumn, but all the other horses
they'd seen that weekend: Misty Morning,
Calypso, Rio and Queenie. She wished there
was more she could do to help horses like
Calypso. She thought of Magic and how his
fate could have been very different.

If she and the Silver Shoe team
hadn't rescued him and brought him to

the stables, who knew what might have happened to him? It was clear he hadn't come from a happy home. When they'd found him he'd been neglected and was in poor condition. Now, he was a fine, healthy horse who had everything going for him.

Tilly could hear her parents downstairs watching TV. She decided to get a cup of hot chocolate. She crept past her brother Adam, who was sound asleep in the room next to hers, and through to the kitchen.

'Hey, Tiger Lil', what you doing?' called her dad.

'Just getting a drink,' she replied.

While she was waiting for the kettle to boil, she opened her dad's laptop, which was lying on the kitchen worktop. She clicked on the internet search icon and typed in 'horse rescue'. One of the first websites that came up was World Horse Welfare, a charity that helped rescue, rehabilitate and rehome horses all around the world. The Silver Shoe gang had helped raise money for them last year,

when they'd put on a talent show with
Nimrod, the ex-circus pony.

She remembered that her school
work experience project was coming up.
World Horse Welfare would be the perfect
placement! She decided to write to them as
soon as she could.

Tilly made her hot chocolate and took it
back to bed. The idea of working for World
Horse Welfare made her feel happy and
distracted her from worries about Mia and
Autumn Glory. Soon she was sound asleep,
dreaming that she and Mia were riding
Magic and Autumn through country lanes.

School seemed to drag on forever the next
day. Tilly and her friend Becky met Mia at
lunchtime, but they decided not to mention
Autumn's name in case they jinxed it. In the
afternoon Tilly had Double Science, which
she normally loved, but today she couldn't

concentrate. All she could think about was whether Mia would get her new horse.

Tilly's dad gave her a lift to Silver Shoe after school. Mia and her parents were driving straight to Stitch Green. When she got there, Tilly went about her usual duties, but even then, she couldn't focus. She nearly put twice the amount of feed in Magic's bucket (which he would have loved!) and tripped over a bale of straw.

'Have you heard anything from Mia yet?' said Angela, as she passed her in the yard.

'Not yet.'

Suddenly she felt her phone buzz. Mia. She answered straightaway, but all she could hear was lots of screaming. It sounded like happy screaming but she couldn't be certain.

'Mia! Slow down, what are you saying?'

'They said yes! We're going to get Autumn Glory! All he needs now is to be vetted! I'm so excited! Can you ask Angela if Brian is free to come and see Autumn today?'

82

Tilly gave Angela a thumbs-up and called her over.

'Slow down, Tilly,' said Angela. 'I'll see if Brian is available, but he'll need to do a thorough examination before Mia's parents go ahead with the purchase. Let's not get carried away just yet.'

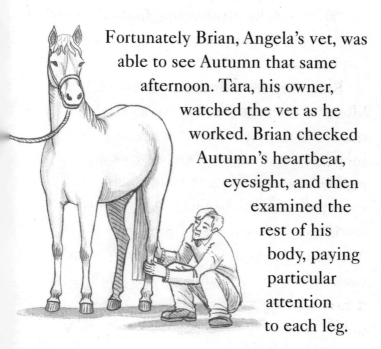

Fortunately Brian, Angela's vet, was able to see Autumn that same afternoon. Tara, his owner, watched the vet as he worked. Brian checked Autumn's heartbeat, eyesight, and then examined the rest of his body, paying particular attention to each leg.

83

Then he trotted him up several times and saw him on a circle.

'You're being very thorough,' said Tara.

'I need to be,' said Brian. 'I wouldn't want Mia's dream to be shattered by a horse with a heart murmur, or something like that. But all thumbs-up, he's passed. I'll let her parents know.'

Early evening at Silver Shoe, as Tilly was getting ready to go home, her phone buzzed for the second time that day.

'I've got my horse! I've got my horse! I'm so happy!'

Listening to Mia's excited shouts, a huge sense of joy and relief washed over Tilly.

'Did you hear that, boy?' she said, walking towards Magic's stable, and stroking his nose. 'You're getting a new friend!'

Ten

Mia and her parents brought Autumn Glory to Silver Shoe at the weekend in a horsebox they'd borrowed from Angela. They pulled into the car park and Tilly was there to meet them.

'How did he travel?' she called out, desperate to catch a glimpse of the new Silver Shoe resident.

'Fine,' said Mia. 'And he was really pleased to see me!'

Together they let the ramp down and

Mia climbed through the little jockey door at the front of the trailer. She greeted Autumn and untied his ropes, then led him quietly down the ramp. He walked out with confidence. He didn't seem at all fazed by the journey, or his new surroundings.

'That's my boy,' said Mia proudly.

Tilly was so happy for her. She couldn't wait to introduce Autumn to Magic.

'I was thinking of going for a hack in a bit.

Do you think Autumn would like some exercise?' she said. 'After his journey?'

'Definitely,' said Mia. 'We'll show him the local scenery, shall we? I'll get him settled then we'll tack up.'

Once Autumn was ready, he and Mia joined Tilly and Magic at the gates. The two horses studied each other inquisitively. They pricked their ears then sniffed and bobbed their noses. Autumn made a blowing noise.

'I think he's saying 'Hello',' said Mia.

'It certainly looks as though they're keen to get to know each other. And maybe now's a good time to give you this,' said Tilly, handing Mia one of the horsehair bracelets she'd made.

'Wow, thanks, Tilly. This is amazing. I'll wear it next to Moonshadow's bracelet. It's so great knowing that Autumn is mine now.

It was exciting going to get him. If only . . .'

Her voice tailed off.

'What's wrong?'

'Oh, I just felt bad. As we were leaving Stitch Green, Tara got really upset. She put on a brave face but I could tell she was gutted. It's obvious how much she loved Autumn. She's really going to miss him.'

'Hmmm,' said Tilly. 'That gives me an idea. When I made your bracelet there were some hairs left over. I twiddled them into a second bracelet. I hadn't really thought about what to do with it.'

'Are you thinking what I'm thinking?' said Mia, a twinkle in her eye.

Tilly grinned.

'Hopefully we'll get to see her again soon.'

They took their favourite route, beneath the blossom trees and across to the bridle path. It was a perfect springtime ride. The sun was shining and the sky was clear. Autumn did everything Mia asked him to. They looked as though they'd been riding together for years.

On their return, approaching the gates of the Silver Shoe yard, Autumn pricked his ears and moved forward keenly, as though he'd spotted something. Then Tilly saw what it was. Tara was there, standing with her mum. She looked up as soon as the girls and their horses walked in. Her eyes were wide with pleasure.

'Hey, Autumn! Hi, Mia! We've just stopped off on the way to my aunt's house. We forgot to give you Autumn's best Newmarket blanket.'

Mia dismounted. She and Tilly quickly took Autumn and Magic's bridles off and put their head collars on, then tied them up.

'Thanks,' said Mia, walking over to Tara.

'He looks really settled already. I hope you don't mind that we came by.'

'Not at all. If you ever want to hang out with us or come and visit Autumn, you're welcome.'

'Cool. I'd love to. I won't miss Autumn half as much if I know I can still see him.'

'You remember my friend Tilly?' said Mia, as Tilly came over to them.

'Yes.'

'You liked her bracelets, didn't you?'

'The horsehair ones? Yes, they're beautiful.'

'I've made one for you,' said Tilly, offering it to her. 'It's from Autumn's tail. Actually, I made two – so I've divided them between you and Mia, sort of like Autumn's past and present owners come together.'

Tara held the bracelet up to the light.

'Wow!' she said. 'I LOVE it!'

She tied it round her wrist and held it out next to Mia's. The three girls smiled.

'Thank you so much,' said Tara.

'We should thank you,' said Mia. 'Autumn is such a lovely horse. I'm so

happy. It's taken a long time for me to find the right one.'

'A very long time,' added Tilly. 'Believe me.'

The girls laughed.

'I'm sure he has a great temperament,' Mia continued. 'But we know it helps that you looked after him so well. We've seen a few horses who haven't got such thoughtful owners.'

They stood quietly for a moment, until Autumn made another gentle blowing sound.

'That means he's contented,' said Tara. 'He obviously likes you.'

'And I like him!' said Mia.

'Well, I guess we'd better get going,' said Tara.

'Remember, you can visit any time you like.'

'Definitely,' said Tara. 'And thanks for the bracelet, Tilly.'

The girls took their horses by their halters. They waved goodbye to Tara, then grinned at one another and walked side-by-side towards the stables. The sun was beginning to set and the sky was pale pink. They didn't speak.

There was no need to say anything. They both knew in their hearts what the other was thinking. This was the beginning of many wonderful times they'd have together with their horses, Magic Spirit and Autumn Glory.

Pippa's Top Tips

Horses can pick up stable vices, like crib-biting, or weaving (when they rock from side to side) if they are bored or confined. Always try to ensure your horse or pony gets daily exercise and turned out to pasture, if possible.

If you have a young horse, try not to stable him close to a horse with one of these habits.

Excessive cribbing will cause damage to your horse's teeth, and pacing may place unnecessary stress on the legs.

If your horse sucks in air when he crib-bites, look out for signs of bloating, because this can lead to colic.

Being a good rider isn't just about technique, it means thinking about your horse, constantly assessing his level, and trying to avoid getting into a situation where you might frighten him, or risk losing his confidence.

Always make sure you and your horse have warmed up sufficiently before you start jumping.

Don't use speed to get over a new spooky fence. A horse must have time to see what he is looking at, and should stay forward, 'listening' to your leg.

Remember to take the time to give your horse or pony a breather if he's working hard. If he starts to puff, just walk him until he gets his breath back, then you can continue.

Being a member of your local Pony Club is a great way to get an all-round grounding – you'll learn lots about general horse management, and benefit from the advice of knowledgeable instructors.

Before purchasing a horse or pony, your vet will need to do a very thorough examination – paying particular attention to the heartbeat, eyesight, and legs (soundness).

For more about Tilly and Silver Shoe Farm –
including pony tips, quizzes and everything
you ever wanted to know about horses –
visit www.tillysponytails.co.uk